MARVEL

CIVIL WAR

CAPTAIN AMERICA

marvelkids.com

In accordance with the U.S. Copyright Act of 1976, the scanning, uploading, and electronic sharing of any part of this book without the permission of the publisher is unlawful piracy and theft of the author's intellectual property. If you would like to use material from the book (other than for review purposes), prior written permission must be obtained by contacting the publisher at permissions@hbgusa.com. Thank you for your support of the author's rights.

Little, Brown and Company

Hachette Book Group
1290 Avenue of the Americas, New York, NY 10104
Visit us at lb-kids.com

Little, Brown and Company is a division of Hachette Book Group, Inc.
The Little, Brown name and logo are trademarks of Hachette Book Group, Inc.

The publisher is not responsible for websites (or their content) that are not owned by the publisher.

First Edition: April 2016

Library of Congress Control Number: 2016932123

ISBN 978-0-316-27139-4

10 9 8 7 6 5 4 3 2 1

CW

Printed in United States of America

MARVEL
CIVIL WAR
CAPTAIN AMERICA

THE RISE OF
CROSSBONES

By Chris Strathearn
Illustrated by Ron Lim, Andy Smith, and Andy Troy
Based on the Screenplay by Christopher Markus & Stephen McFeely
Produced by Kevin Feige
Directed by Anthony and Joe Russo

LITTLE, BROWN AND COMPANY
New York Boston

Captain America, Scarlet Witch, Falcon, and Black Widow spy on hired mercenaries in Nigeria. The Avengers know that an attack is being planned here, and they must try to stop it.

"What do you see?" asks Cap.

Natasha, the Black Widow, talks to Wanda, also known as Scarlet Witch.

"The Institute is being watched by that red SUV," says Wanda. "I could move it with my mind."

"It's a bulletproof truck filled with armed men," replies Natasha. "Powers are great, but you still have to look over your shoulder. Watch out for the garbage truck, too."

Falcon, waiting on the roof above, also watches the street.

"I'm sending in my Redwing drone to get a better look!"

The drone is equipped with X-ray cameras that reveal what the garbage truck is hiding.

Captain America also recognizes the danger immediately.

"Everyone, get moving!" yells Cap.

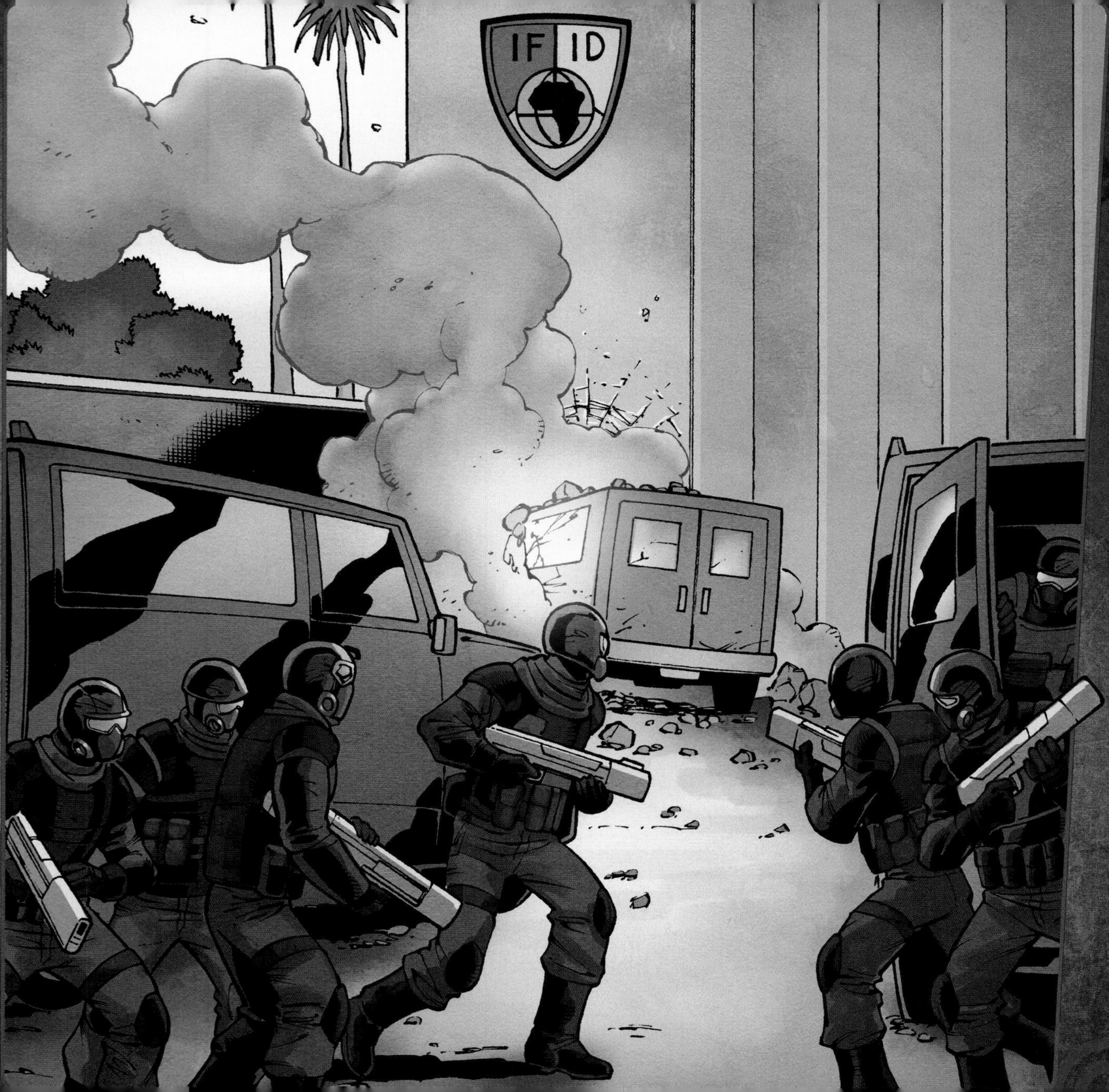
IF ID

With a thundering boom, the truck hits the laboratory building and breaks through the front courtyard wall.

Mercenaries pour out from trucks all over the street. Smoke and gas grenades are thrown at the Institute's guards.

Falcon prepares for action. He is determined to stop the mercenearies!

Making their way into the courtyard, Cap and Wanda begin to repel the attack.

Wanda uses her magic to deflect bullets and fling armed men away.

"We need eyes in the sky!" shouts Cap.

The Redwing drone and its X-ray vision look into the building toward the laboratory.

"There's movement up on the third floor! They're leaving the building!" says Falcon to Cap.

Captain America bursts through a window. He will have to fight his way through the lab.

Captain America finally finds the leader. Crossbones is calling the shots! His face is covered with a skull mask. After fleeing the lab, he fights Captain America to a standstill in the street.

But Cap is finally able to gain the upper hand!
He uses his shield to knock Crossbones down.

Crossbones has had enough.
He makes his move to escape!

Cap radios his team. He knows why Crossbones attacked the lab. "He stole a deadly virus!" Cap reports. "We need to stop him."

"On it," Natasha responds.

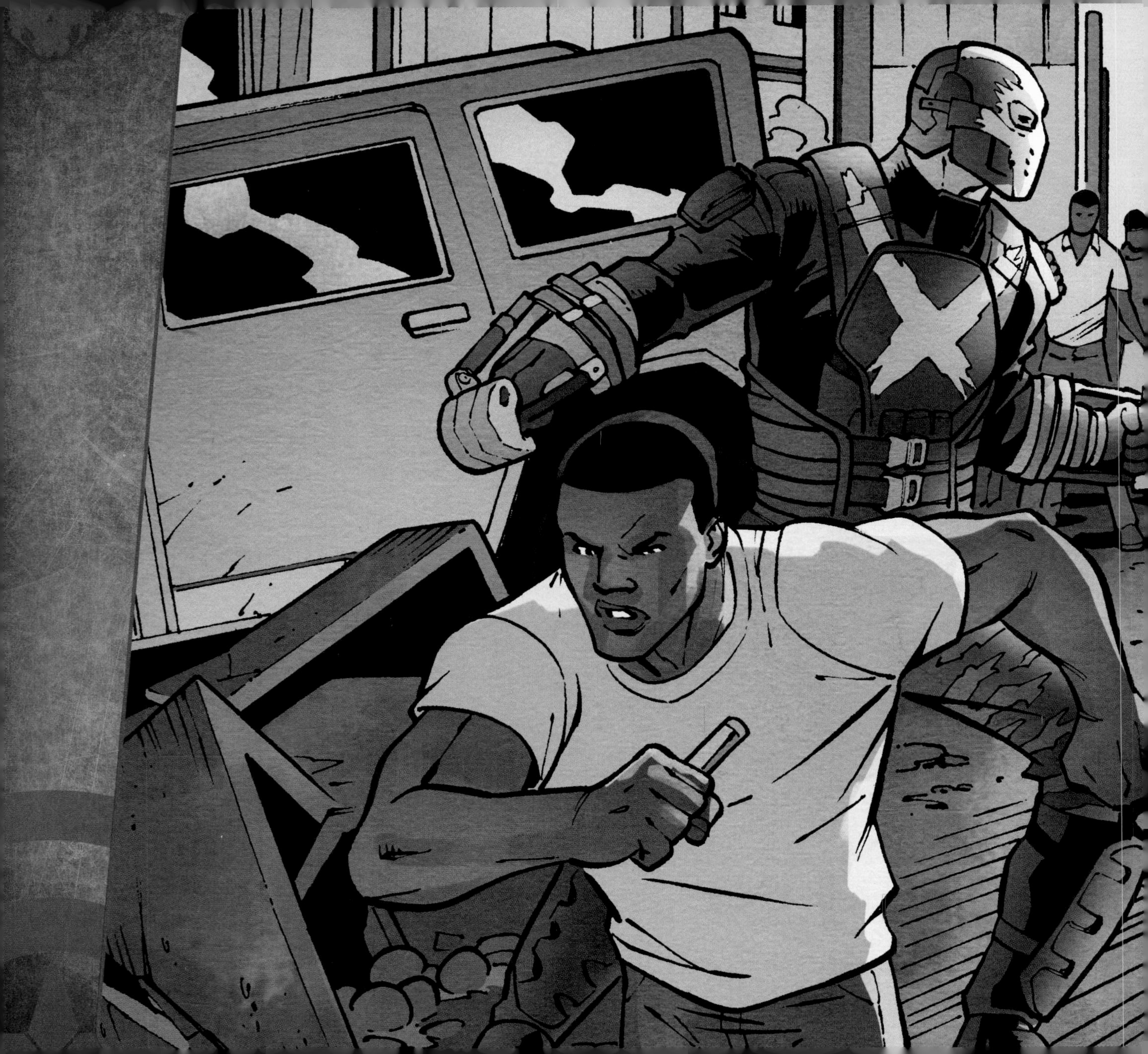

Cap grabs a motorcycle, and the team chases after Crossbones! Crossbones is smart. At first, he tries to lose the Avengers in the crowd. But Falcon can track him from the sky. They're closing in on him, and Crossbones is desperate.

As Falcon races to catch up, Crossbones leaps at Captain America. With his power gauntlets, Crossbones is nearly able to take Cap out before Falcon can get there.

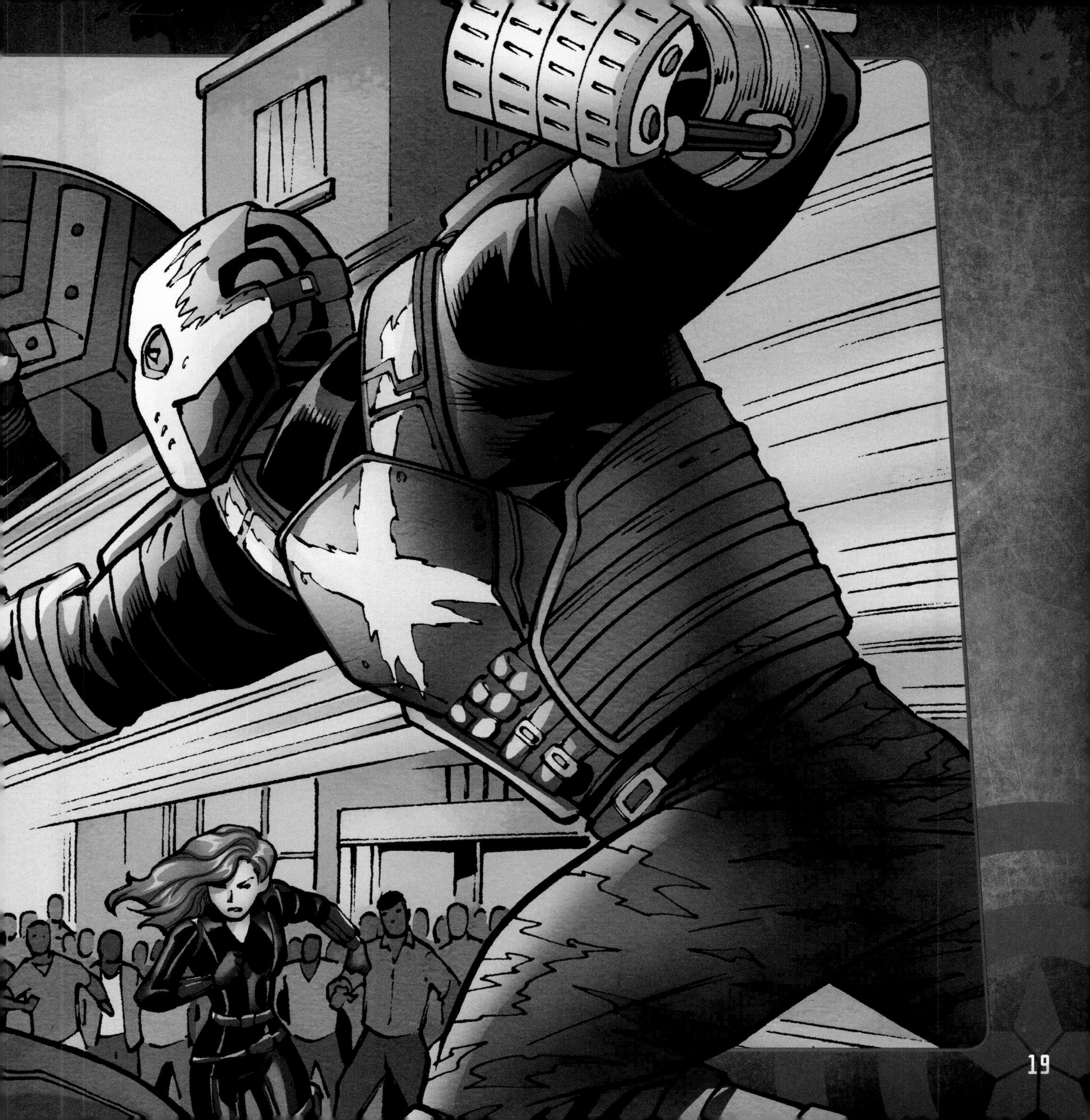

Natasha is not far behind. She is mopping up some of Crossbones's men, searching for the stolen virus.

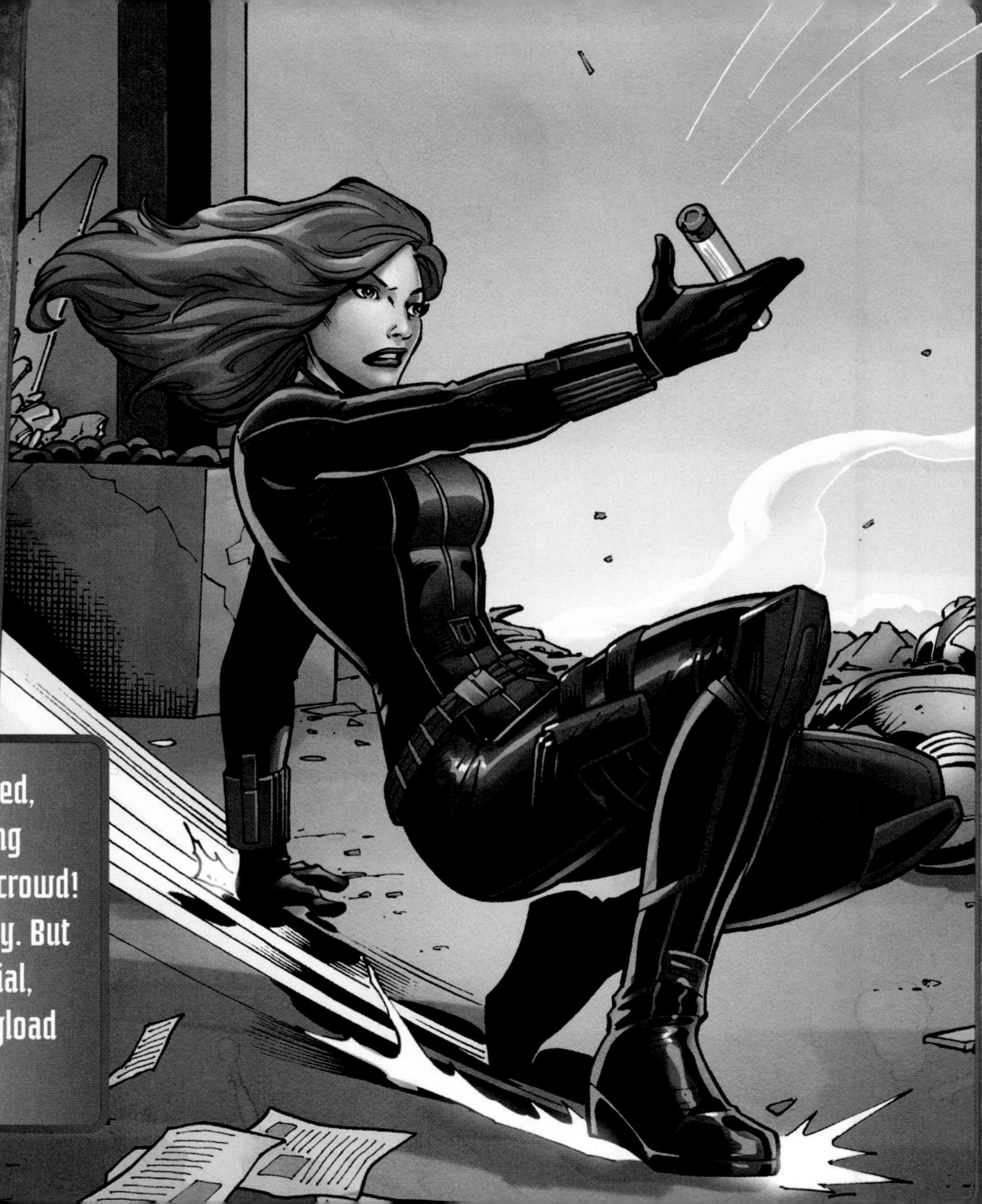

Knowing he will be arrested, the thug with the vial holding the virus throws it into the crowd! People scramble to get away. But Natasha races toward the vial, catching it just in time. "Payload secure," she reports.

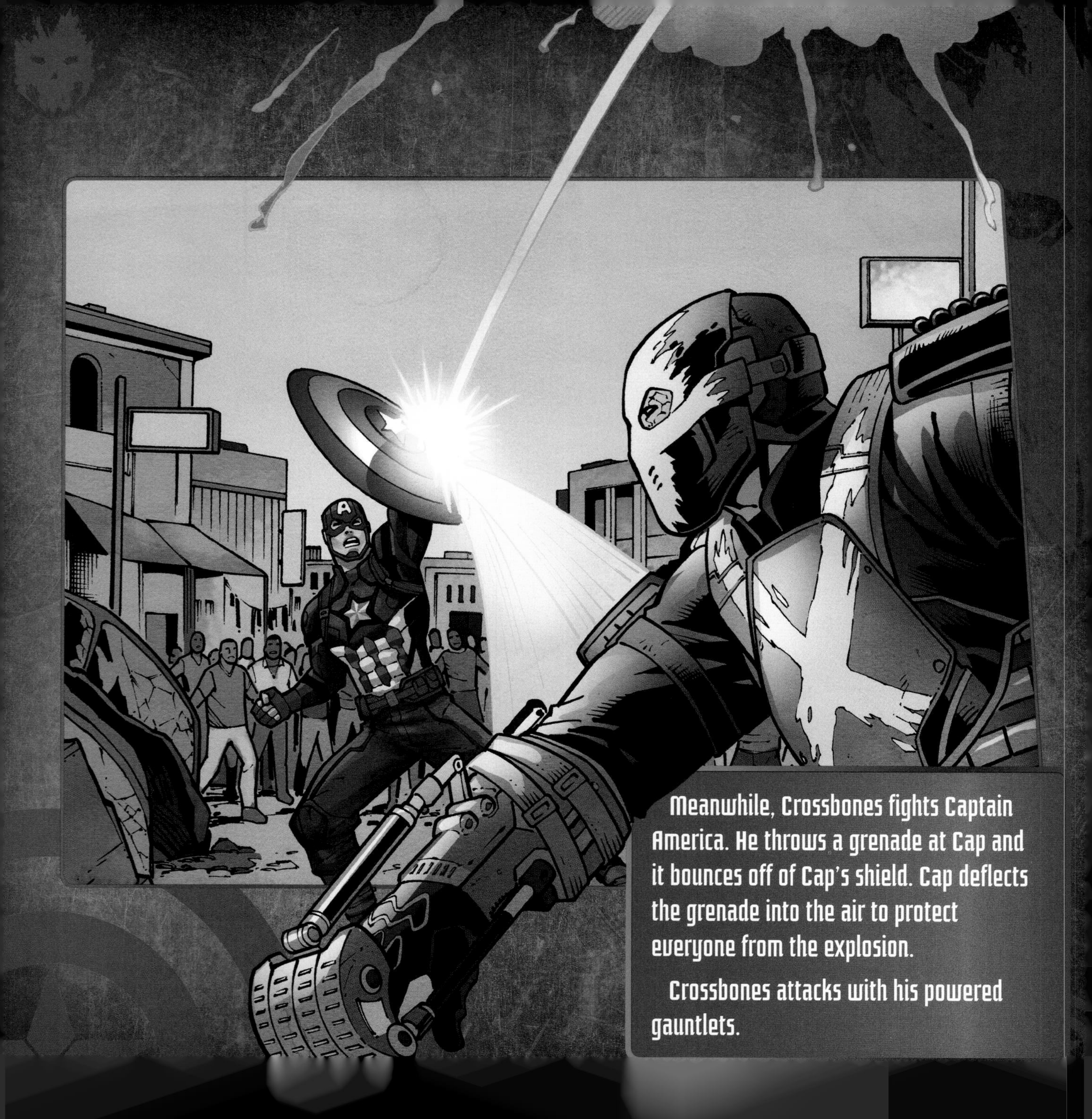

Meanwhile, Crossbones fights Captain America. He throws a grenade at Cap and it bounces off of Cap's shield. Cap deflects the grenade into the air to protect everyone from the explosion.

Crossbones attacks with his powered gauntlets.

Almost beaten, Crossbones triggers an explosive device.

Cap covers himself, expecting to feel the force of the blast. But suddenly, it stops!

Behind him, Wanda is using her powers to contain the explosion.

Cap spins Crossbones around and hits him hard against a wall, and Crossbones's mask shatters! Crossbones is defeated!

Captain America and the Avengers have saved the world from a deadly attack.

But some people think that the destruction that follows them makes the Avengers too dangerous. Iron Man believes that they can't follow their own rules anymore.

But Captain America isn't so sure. He trusts himself to make the right choices.